BUILD YOUR OWN
WEB SITE

Asha Kalbag

Design and DTP   Additional help

Design and DTP:
Russell Punter
Michael Wheatley
Zöe Wray

Cover design by
Isaac Quaye

Managing designer:
Stephen Wright

Technical consultant:
Liam Devany

Additional consultancy by
Artemis Interactive

Photography by
Howard Allman

Edited by Philippa Wingate
and Jane Chisholm

About this book

The World Wide Web, or the Web, is the most exciting part of the Internet. It contains information on all kinds of subjects which is presented in a variety of interesting ways, including words, pictures, animations, sounds and video. Every day, more and more people add information to the Web by setting up or "building" their own Web site.

What is a Web site?

The information on the Web is contained in millions of computer documents, known as Web pages, which you look at on a computer screen. Every Web page has a unique address known as its Uniform Resource Locator (URL). A URL specifies exactly where on the Web a page is stored so it can be found easily.

A Web site is a group of Web pages created by a person or organization. The pages on a Web site are all linked together. You can move from one page to another by clicking on words and pictures called hyperlinks.

This book shows you the two different methods you can use to build your Web site, and explains exactly how to prepare pictures, sounds and animations to include on it. It also tells you how to transfer your site from your computer to the Web.

Building a Web site

One way to create your site is by using a computer code called Hypertext MarkUp Language (HTML), which you can learn from this book.

If you decide to learn HTML, you will probably not need any new software. All you need to create a Web site with HTML is a word processing program or a text editor. Most computers come with a text editor already installed. For example, Microsoft Windows® 95 includes one called Notepad, and most Macs have one called SimpleText.

If you don't want to learn HTML, you will need a program called a Web editor. There are many different Web editors available and you can order one or download one from the Internet. (Find out more about Web editors on pages 6 and 7.)

Whichever method you use to build your Web site, you will need a computer with an Internet connection and a program called a browser.

A browser

A browser is a program that allows you to look at Web pages. One of the most popular browsers is called Netscape Navigator®. It is used for the examples in this book. You can find out how to obtain Netscape Navigator on pages 40 and 41.

Don't worry if you already have another browser, such as Microsoft® Internet Explorer. Most browsers are very similar. Using the examples in this book as a guide, you will be able to work out how to use your own browser in the same way.

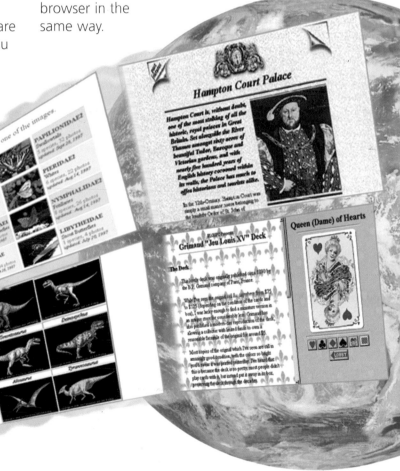

Why build a Web site?

Each person or organization that creates a Web site wants to share information with millions of other Web users. Here are some of the reasons why people put information on the Web.

Be known worldwide

Individual Net users build Web sites to tell others about themselves, their families and friends. They often include information about their hobbies and interests.

Publish a fanzine

Fans and enthusiasts devote their Web pages to celebrities, pop groups, movies or TV shows of their choice. There are fanzines for all kinds of famous people, including sportsmen and women, film stars, TV actors and comedians. They contain stories, photographs, sound clips, videos and trivia for other fans to enjoy.

A site devoted to a pop group

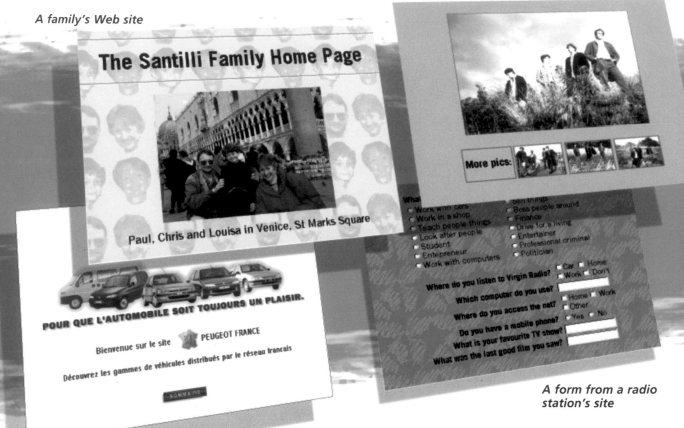

A family's Web site

The Santilli Family Home Page

Paul, Chris and Louisa in Venice, St Marks Square

POUR QUE L'AUTOMOBILE SOIT TOUJOURS UN PLAISIR.

Bienvenue sur le site   PEUGEOT FRANCE

Découvrez les gammes de véhicules distribués par le réseau francais

SOMMAIRE

A car manufacturer's site

More pics:

What
Work with cars   Sell things
Work in a shop   Boss people around
Teach people things   Finance
Look after people   Drive for a living
Student   Entertainer
Entrepreneur   Professional criminal
Work with computers   Politician

Where do you listen to Virgin Radio?
Which computer do you use?
Where do you access the net?
Do you have a mobile phone?
What is your favourite TV show?
What was the last good film you saw?

A form from a radio station's site

Make contact

All sorts of organizations use the Web to find out about other Web users. For example, companies often include forms on their sites to discover their customers' preferences and opinions. Companies can use the information they collect to make improvements to their products or services.

Advertise and sell things

Web sites are a great way for companies to provide up-to-date information about their products and services. Many commercial sites contain forms that customers can use to order and pay for the things that are advertised.

Have fun

Entertainment companies use the Web to promote TV shows, movies and musicians. News updates, pictures, sound clips and short videos keep fans informed and entertained. There are also sites built by individuals with jokes, puzzles, cartoons, games and stories.

Share knowledge

Researchers, students and specialists in every field build Web sites to share useful information. From recipes to medical advice, academic articles to drawing techniques, there is a wealth of free information on the Web.

A TV show's Web site

A site where children can obtain help with their homework

A Web site for a charity that helps children all over the world

A Web site about the Swedish Royal family

Support a cause

Charities, political parties and religious organizations use Web sites to explain their goals and beliefs. Many of these sites contain details of an organization's campaigns and achievements. A site may also include instructions for people who want to send money or get involved.

Promote a country

Government Web sites inform Web users about the different activities of the various government bodies.

Different government sites have different functions. For example, there are sites that encourage tourism, sites that explain where people can get help with legal or health problems, and sites where people can find out about public figures, such as politicians.

Web editors

A Web editor is a program that helps you create Web pages. It automatically produces HTML, the computer code that turns ordinary documents into Web pages. The advantage of using a Web editor is that you don't have to learn HTML to build your Web site.

This section shows you how to use two different types of Web editors. There is also some advice about obtaining a Web editor.

WYSIWYG Web editors

The most popular type of Web editors are known as WYSIWYG Web editors. WYSIWYG stands for "What you see is what you get". As you build Web pages with a WYSIWYG Web editor, it shows you what they will look like when they are viewed through a browser. You will see all the words, pictures and animations that you have included on your page.

Using a WYSIWYG Web editor

With a WYSIWYG Web editor, you start by typing some text into a blank document. You can insert files created in other programs, such as pictures, animations and sounds, whenever you want to.

Once you have created a basic page, you can reorganize the information on it by dragging pieces of text or pictures into a new position. There are various buttons and menu items that you can use to improve your page's appearance. For example, to change the way a word looks, you can select it with your mouse and click on a button that makes it bold or italic or underlines it.

As you build up a page, a Web editor automatically produces the HTML code that enables a browser to understand and display the information correctly.

A WYSIWYG editor called Microsoft® FrontPage® Express

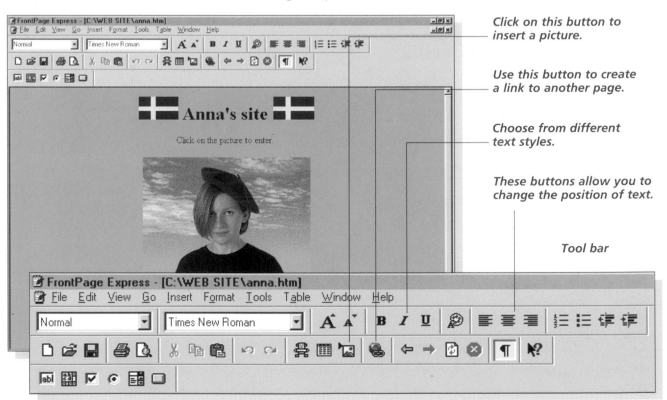

Click on this button to insert a picture.

Use this button to create a link to another page.

Choose from different text styles.

These buttons allow you to change the position of text.

Tool bar

Building with blocks

Some Web editors, such as Hotdog Express, work differently. Hotdog Express is designed specially for beginners. It uses blocks that represent a part of a Web page, such as a paragraph of text, a picture or a horizontal line.

To build up a Web page, you place the blocks in the order you wish the different parts to appear. You use a dialog box to specify what you want a particular image or piece of text to look like. At any time, you can instruct Hotdog Express to show you what your page will look like on the Web.

Hotdog Express

Use this screen to build up a Web page.

Click here to see a preview.

This is a preview of the Web page the program has produced.

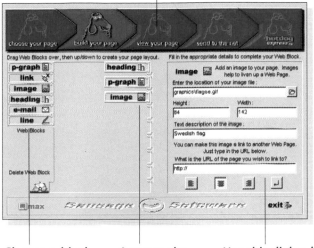

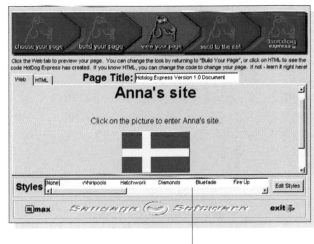

Choose a block from here.

Arrange the blocks here.

Use this dialog box to give details about each part of your page.

Use this section to select a background for your page.

Obtaining a Web editor

Here is some information that will help you get hold of a Web editor:

Where can I find a Web editor?
On page 41, there is a list of Web sites from which you can order or download Web editors. Alternatively, you can use a "search engine" to find similar sites. This is a program which searches the Web for pages containing a particular word or words, such as **Web editor**. There is a list of search engines on page 43.

How much will it cost?
Some Web editors are free of charge. For example, Microsoft FrontPage Express, shown on page 6, comes free with Microsoft's browser, Internet Explorer 4.0. You can also obtain a Web editor called Netscape Composer for free from the Internet.

There are also many Web editors that you have to pay for, but you can try out most of them free of charge for a limited period. It is a good idea to test several different programs in this way before you spend any money.

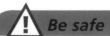

Planning your Web site

Before you start building a Web site, you should plan it carefully. Decide what sort of information you are going to include, and how you are going to organize it. Before you use your computer, jot down your ideas on paper so that you can work out the best way of presenting them.

⚠️ Be safe

Millions of Web users will be able to see the information on your Web site. Don't include anything private, such as your home address or telephone number.

Decide content

With the Web, you aren't restricted to using words to share information with other people. You can use sounds and pictures too. For example, if you are a musician, you could include a short recording of your music. If you belong to a club, you could use photographs to introduce its members, or to show the sort of activities it arranges. You could also add a chart detailing future events.

You can also use photographs or pictures created on a computer to decorate your Web pages. Pictures created on a computer are known as computer graphics.

Organize content

Decide how many pages your Web site is going to contain and divide up your content between them. Give each page a title which indicates the information it will contain, for example, "About Usborne Publishing" or "Computer Guides". This will help you decide where each piece of information fits best.

How long?

Don't try to put too much information on one page. There should be enough content to fill at least one screen. But if you have to scroll down more than two screens to reach the bottom of a page, you should divide up the information into a few shorter pages instead.

Here are some of the things that you can include on your Web site.

Sounds – Find out how to insert sounds on page 27.

Backgrounds – Discover how to add attractive backgrounds on page 23.

Hyperlinks – Page 25 explains how to include picture links.

Photographs – Learn how to include photographs on page 22.

Design a layout

It is a good idea to design your Web site on paper first. Making sketches like the ones shown above will help you decide where to put pictures in relation to text.

Include a home page

Once you know what you are going to put on your site, you can plan a "home page". This is an introductory page which tells visitors what information your site contains. It can also include information such as when a site was built or updated.

A home page

This picture links to a page about music.

This one links to a page containing photographs.

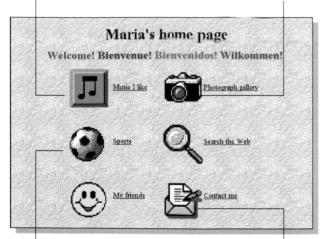

Follow this link to see a page about soccer.

Click here to send a message to the creator of the site.

Type in your information

Once you have planned your Web site on paper, you need to start putting the information into your computer. The program you will use for this depends on which of the methods for building Web sites you have chosen (see pages 2 and 3).

If you have decided not to learn HTML, you will need to use a Web editor.

If you have decided to learn HTML, you can type the information in any text editor or word processing program.

Either way, you should always create a separate document for each of your pages.

Saving a Web page

Even a small Web site can be made up of several files. You may want to create a new directory or folder on your computer's hard disk where you can save each file as you create it. Each file should have a name that is no more than eight letters and numbers long.

If you are using a Web editor, it will automatically save your work as a Web page when you use the *Save* button or menu item.

If you are using a text editor or word processing program, you need to instruct it how to save your work by entering particular information into the Save As dialog box. First make sure *Plain Text* or *Text Documents* is selected in the *Save file as type* field. To specify that the file is a Web page, add the file extension **.htm** to the filename.

Notepad's Save As dialog box

Many people call their home page "index".

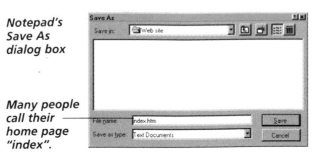

HTML

<HEAD> <TITLE> <BODY>

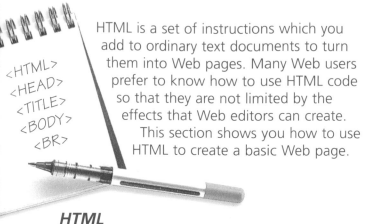

HTML is a set of instructions which you add to ordinary text documents to turn them into Web pages. Many Web users prefer to know how to use HTML code so that they are not limited by the effects that Web editors can create. This section shows you how to use HTML to create a basic Web page.

HTML

HTML instructions tell a browser that a document is a Web page, and how the information on it should be displayed. For example, there are HTML instructions which tell a browser where to place the text on the page. There are other HTML instructions which dictate how the words should appear.

Tags

An HTML instruction is called a tag. Tags usually come in pairs – an opening part and a closing part. The opening part comes before the words that are affected by the instruction, and the closing part goes after them. In this example, the tag affects the word "Maria".

Opening part  *Closing part*

`<B>` Maria `</B>`

Each part of a tag is put inside these two symbols: < >. They are known as angle brackets. In the example, B instructs a browser to display Maria in bold type. The closing part of a tag always includes a forward slash </ >.

You can type tags in capital letters or small letters. However, it's a good idea to use capital letters so that the tags stand out from the content of a document. This makes it easier to find and alter tags when you want to make changes to your Web pages.

A Web page source document

Connect your computer to the Internet and download a Web page. Notice that you can't see any HTML tags when you look at a Web page through a browser.

The HTML for a particular Web page is known as its source document. To see the source document of a Web page, select *Page Source* from the *View* menu. Don't be scared by what you see. HTML looks confusing but it's quite easy to use.

Yahoo!'s home page and its source

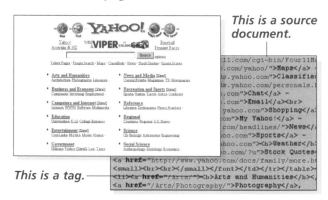

This is a source document.

This is a tag.

A universal code

HTML is "platform-independent". This means that any type of computer can understand it. It doesn't matter what kind of computer is used to write it. If you have a Mac, you can look at a Web page that was created on an IBM compatible PC.

An IBM compatible PC and a Mac displaying the same Web page

PC　　　*Mac*

Essential code

Some essential tags appear in every source document. The tags shown below must appear at the top of a document.

```
<HTML>
<HEAD>
<TITLE>        page title        </TITLE>
</HEAD>
<BODY>
```

In your text editor, open up your home page document. Type the above sequence of tags at the top. Choose a suitable title for your page, for example "Maria's home page", and type it where the words "page title" appear above. Next, type these two tags at the bottom of your document:

```
</BODY>
</HTML>
```

When you have finished, save your document. It should now look similar to the source document shown below.

Using your browser

You can now look at your document through your browser. To do this, start your browser without connecting to the Internet. Select *Open Page...* from the *File* menu. Click on the *Choose File...* button. Use the dialog box that appears to find your document, then highlight its name and click *Open*. Your document will appear inside your browser window as a Web page, similar to the one in the picture below.

Other tags

Over the next pages, you will discover some tags that enable you to change the appearance of the words on a Web page, and to add pictures, sounds and hyperlinks.

To add any of these tags to your source document, open it with your text editor. When you have finished making changes, save the file. You can see the changes by opening the file in your browser again, or by clicking on your browser's *Reload* button.

A source document and the Web page it produces

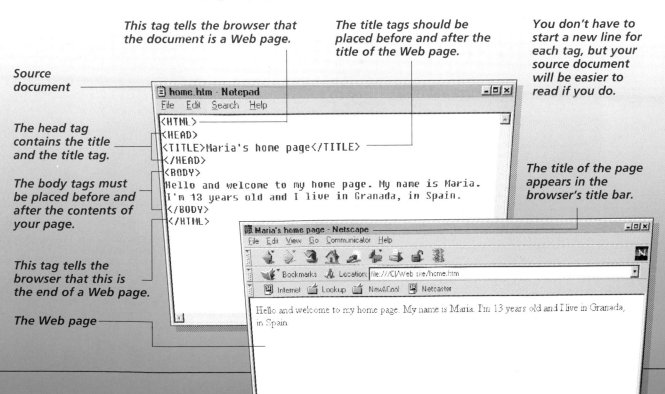

This tag tells the browser that the document is a Web page.

The title tags should be placed before and after the title of the Web page.

You don't have to start a new line for each tag, but your source document will be easier to read if you do.

Source document

The head tag contains the title and the title tag.

The body tags must be placed before and after the contents of your page.

This tag tells the browser that this is the end of a Web page.

The Web page

The title of the page appears in the browser's title bar.

Special effects with text

These pages show you some tags that change the appearance of the text on a Web page.

Dividing up text

It is difficult to read large amounts of text on a computer screen. To make it easier for Web users to look at your page, you should divide up long pieces of text into smaller sections.

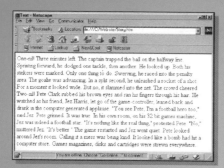

Large areas of text on a Web page look dull and are hard to read.

You can divide up text by instructing a browser to start a new paragraph or a new line. The tags that you use to do this have only one part. They are known as standalones.

To tell a browser to start a new paragraph, type <P> in front of the first word of the paragraph in the source document. Browsers display a blank line between two paragraphs.

To tell a browser to start a new line, type <BR> where you want it to begin.

A source document and its Web page

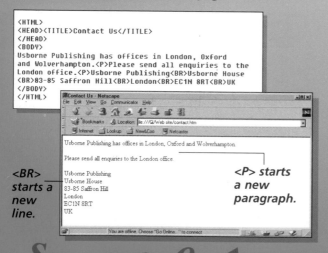

*
 starts a new line.*

<P> starts a new paragraph.

White space

It is easier to work with a source document that contains plenty of white space. You can use the Return key as often as you like to create white space in your source documents. This will not affect the appearance of your Web pages. Browsers will only break up the text on Web pages when they are instructed to do so by tags.

Both these source documents produce the same Web page.

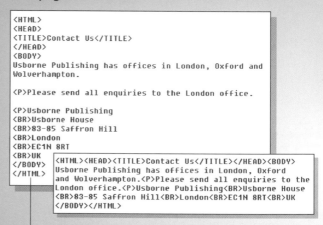

This source is much easier to read.

Emphasizing text

You can use bold and italic type to make important words on your page stand out from the rest of the text.

Your text editor may contain buttons or menu items that convert words into bold or italic type. However, when a browser displays a Web page, it ignores any special effects created using these tools. It will only recognize instructions that are given in HTML.

To instruct a browser to display a piece of text in bold type, type <B> before the text and </B> after it, like this:<B>Usborne</B>.

To instruct a browser to display a piece of text in italic type, type <I> before the text and </I> after it, like this: <I>Usborne</I>.

Letter size

You can also emphasize a word by altering the size of its letters. There are seven letter sizes, known as font sizes, to choose from. Size 1 is the smallest and size 7 is the biggest.

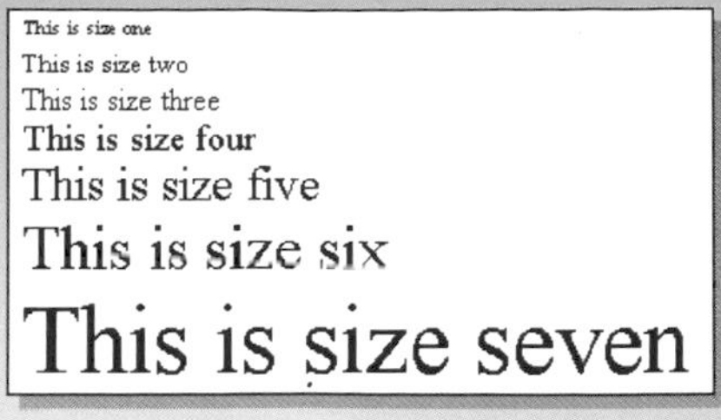

This is size one
This is size two
This is size three
This is size four
This is size five
This is size six
This is size seven

This picture compares the seven font sizes.

To change a section of text into size 6 font, you would type <FONT SIZE="6"> in front of it and </FONT> after it. To use a different font size, simply replace 6 with another number.

Heading

It is a good idea to use headings to introduce the different sections of text on a Web page. Headings help visitors to your site find information that interests them quickly.

There are six sizes of headings. Level 1 is the biggest and level 6 is the smallest. Levels 1, 2 and 3 are usually used for titles.

Using headings helps divide up text.

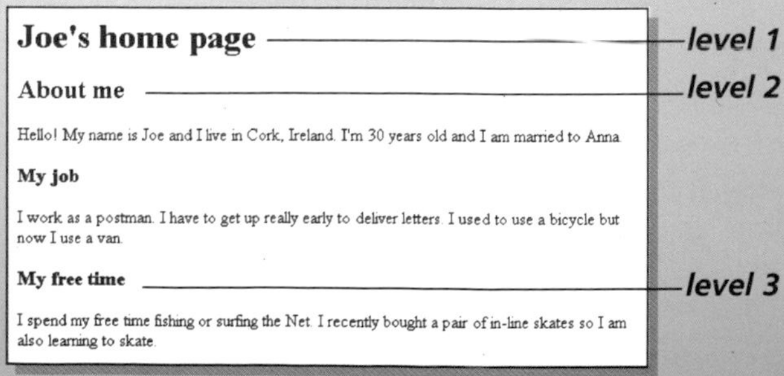

Joe's home page ——————————— *level 1*

About me ——————————————— *level 2*

Hello! My name is Joe and I live in Cork, Ireland. I'm 30 years old and I am married to Anna.

My job

I work as a postman. I have to get up really early to deliver letters. I used to use a bicycle but now I use a van.

My free time ——————————— *level 3*

I spend my free time fishing or surfing the Net. I recently bought a pair of in-line skates so I am also learning to skate.

To turn a piece of text into a level 1 heading, type <H1> in front of the text and </H1> after it. For other heading levels, use the same tag but replace 1 with the appropriate number.

Which tag?

Although both heading tags and <FONT SIZE> tags change the size of text, they aren't interchangeable.

A heading tag should only be used to change the size of section headings. It belongs to a group of tags known as block level elements. Browsers automatically leave blank lines after block level elements.

A <FONT SIZE> tag should be used for all other text. It belongs to a group of tags known as text level elements. These tags affect only the look of the text, not its position on the page.

You can find lists of other block level and text level elements on Web sites that tell you more about HTML (see page 43).

Combining tags

When you place more than one tag around a piece of text, it is important to insert the tags in the correct order, as shown below.

Two tags placed correctly

A tag can contain another tag.

<H1> <I> ASHA </I> </H1>

Two tags placed incorrectly

Tags must not overlap each other.

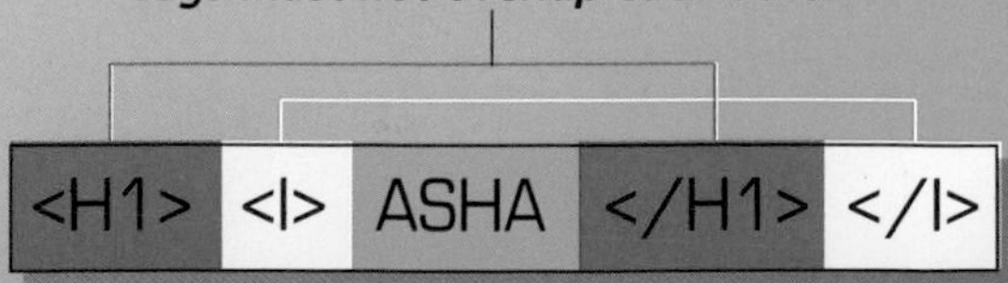

<H1> <I> ASHA </H1> </I>

Block level elements can contain other block level elements or text level elements. Text level elements can only contain other text level elements.

Colour

Unless instructed otherwise, a browser will display text in black on a grey or white background. To make your Web site look more attractive, you can specify different colours for the background and the text.

Describing colours

When people describe colours, they use adjectives such as light, dark and bright to distinguish between different shades. A computer, on the other hand, describes colours using combinations of letters and numbers known as hexadecimal colour codes. These codes are always made up of 6 characters. For example, the code 000000 describes black.

A tag that instructs a browser to use a particular colour must always contain a hexadecimal colour code.

Colour codes

You can find addresses of Web sites that list hexadecimal codes on page 41, but here are a few to get you started:

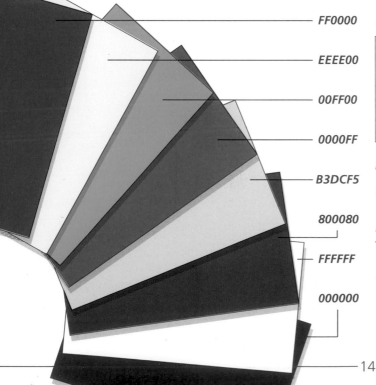

FF0000

EEEE00

00FF00

0000FF

B3DCF5

800080

FFFFFF

000000

How many colours?

It is estimated that hexadecimal codes can describe around 16 million different colours but most computers can't show this many.

The number of colours a computer monitor can show depends on the type of video card inside the processing unit. Most Web users have computers that contain 8-bit or 16-bit video cards. An 8-bit card can display 256 colours and a 16-bit card can display 65,536.

If a computer can't display the exact shade specified in a source document, it will show the nearest colour that it can display.

Background

To change the background colour of a Web page, you need to insert some extra code into the opening part of its <BODY> tag.

Imagine you want the background of a page to be the shade of blue which is described by the code 87CEEB. If you replace <BODY> with <BODY BGCOLOR="#87CEEB">, your browser will display the page with a blue background.

This picture shows a source and the Web page with a coloured background that it produces.

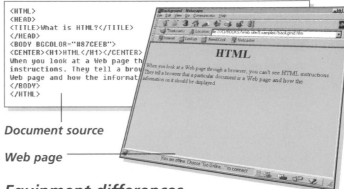

Document source

Web page

Equipment differences

Colours appear brighter on a Mac computer than on an IBM compatible PC. A Web page designed on a Mac will appear slightly duller on a PC.

Text colour

You can change the colour of all the text on a page by adding some code to the <BODY> tag. For example, to instruct a browser to display the text on a page in red, add TEXT= "#FF0000" to the opening part of the body tag, as follows: <BODY TEXT= "#FF0000">. The closing part of the tag remains unchanged.

Highlight a section of text

You can instruct a browser to display a section of text, a word or a single letter in a particular colour. For example, to turn a piece of text blue, type <FONT COLOR="#0000FF"> in front of the text that you want to change. Then type </FONT> after this text to close the tag. The rest of the text on the page won't be affected.

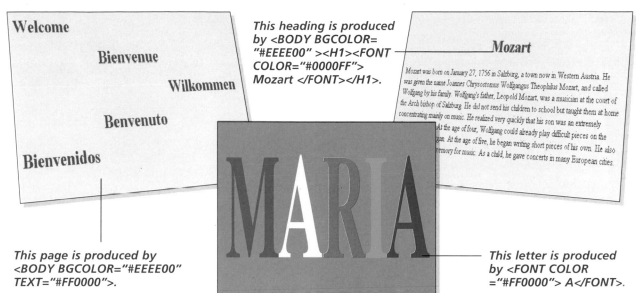

This heading is produced by <BODY BGCOLOR= "#EEEE00" ><H1><FONT COLOR="#0000FF"> Mozart </FONT></H1>.

Mozart

Mozart was born on January 27, 1756 in Salzburg, a town now in Western Austria. He was given the name Joannes Chrysostomus Wolfgangus Theophilus Mozart, and called Wolfgang by his family. Wolfgang's father, Leopold Mozart, was a musician at the court of the Arch bishop of Salzburg. He did not send his children to school but taught them at home concentrating mainly on music. He realized very quickly that his son was an extremely ... At the age of four, Wolfgang could already play difficult pieces on the ...gan. At the age of five, he began writing short pieces of his own. He also ...memory for music. As a child, he gave concerts in many European cities.

This page is produced by <BODY BGCOLOR="#EEEE00" TEXT="#FF0000">.

This letter is produced by <FONT COLOR ="#FF0000"> A</FONT>.

Colour advice

It is fun to experiment with different text and background colours. However, before you settle for a particular combination, make sure that all the text on your page is easy to read. Dark colours, such as navy blue or black, look good on a white or pastel background. Light colours, such as white or yellow, show up clearly on a dark background.

Avoid large amounts of very bright colours such as red (FF0000) or shocking pink (FF69B4). People may not bother to explore your site thoroughly if you make it difficult for them to read the information it contains.

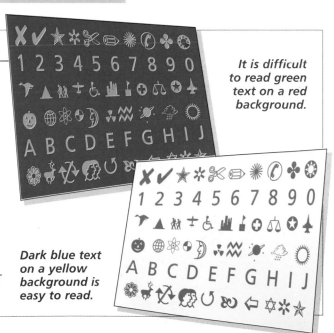

It is difficult to read green text on a red background.

Dark blue text on a yellow background is easy to read.

Organizing information

You can use a variety of devices, such as lists or lines, to organize the text on a Web page.

Lists

There are three types of lists that you can include on a Web site: ordered lists, unordered lists and definition lists.

Ordered lists

You should create an ordered list when the items in your list need to appear in a particular order, for instance, classes on a timetable.

Type <OL> before the text which you want to turn into an ordered list and </OL> after it. Then type <LI> in front of each item in the list. Browsers will display a number in front of each item, as shown in the picture below.

The code for the list shown below is: <OL><LI>English<LI>Biology<LI>Physics<LI>German<LI>Art<LI>History<LI>Geography</OL>.

If you add another item anywhere in an ordered list, browsers will automatically renumber all the items appropriately.

An ordered list

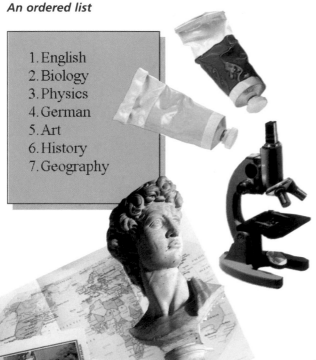

1. English
2. Biology
3. Physics
4. German
5. Art
6. History
7. Geography

Unordered lists

Use an unordered list for items of equal importance, such as items in a shopping list.

To create an unordered list, type <UL> before the text and </UL> after it. Then type <LI> in front of each item in the list. For example, <UL><LI>strawberry<LI>blackberry<LI>lemon<LI>apple<LI>plum</UL>. Browsers will display a dot known as a bullet point in front of each item.

An unordered list

- strawberry
- blackberry
- lemon
- apple
- plum

Definition lists

A definition list is ideal for a collection of words and their meanings, such as a glossary.

To create a definition list, type <DL> before all the text and </DL> after it. Then type <DT> in front of each term that is defined and <DD> in front of each definition. Browsers display each definition on a new line.

The code for the definition list shown here is: <DL><DT>Winter<DD>The coldest season of the year<DT>Summer<DD>The warmest season of the year</DL>.

A definition list

Winter
    The coldest season of the year
Summer
    The warmest season of the year

Quotations

A block quote tag tells browsers to separate a particular section of text from the other text on a Web page. It is often used to indicate quotations which are words written or said by somebody else.

A block quote tag places text in the middle of a page.

Here is a quote from Hamlet:

    To be or not to be,
    That is the question.

Hamlet was written by William Shakespeare in the 16th century.

To turn a piece of text into a block quote, type <BLOCKQUOTE> before it and </BLOCKQUOTE> after it.

Arranging text

Browsers can line text up with the left or right side of a page. This is known as aligning text.

Aligned text

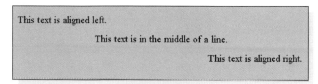

This text is aligned left.

        This text is in the middle of a line.

                This text is aligned right.

To align a piece of text, you need to insert an extra instruction in the <P> or heading tag that appears before it (see pages 12-13).
For example, if you want to align text left, type <P ALIGN="LEFT">. To align text right, type RIGHT instead of LEFT.

Browsers can also place text in the middle of a line. To instruct a browser to do this, type <CENTER> in front of the text and </CENTER> after the text. For example <CENTER>This text is in the middle of a line </CENTER>.

Horizontal lines

Horizontal lines or "rules" can be used to divide up your page into sections. To insert a horizontal rule, you use a standalone tag: <HR>. Type this tag wherever you want a rule to appear. Browsers automatically display a thin rule that extends all the way across a Web page.

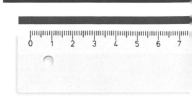

You can change a rule's appearance by adding extra information to its <HR> tag. For example, to instruct a browser to display a rule that is half as wide as a page, type <HR WIDTH="50%">. (You can change the percentage as required.)

To change a rule's thickness, type: <HR SIZE =?>, replacing ? with a number. The higher the number, the thicker the rule.

Browsers automatically place rules in the middle of a line. To alter a rule's position, add ALIGN="LEFT" or ALIGN="RIGHT" to its <HR> tag. Try out different instructions to find a rule that looks good on your page.

A variety of horizontal rules

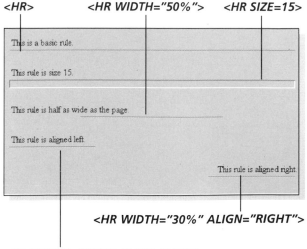

<HR> **<HR WIDTH="50%">** **<HR SIZE=15>**

This is a basic rule.

This rule is size 15.

This rule is half as wide as the page.

This rule is aligned left.

                This rule is aligned right.

<HR WIDTH="30%" ALIGN="RIGHT">

<HR WIDTH="30%" ALIGN="LEFT">

Pictures on the Web

One of the reasons the Web is such a popular source of information is because it contains pictures. Here are some of the ways in which pictures can be used on a Web site.

A picture gallery

Some Web sites contain a gallery section where pictures are displayed. This may include a page of "thumbnails", which are small versions of the images that are displayed elsewhere on the site. If you decide you want to see a larger version of a picture, you can click on its thumbnail to download it.

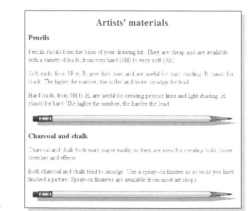

A page of thumbnails

Click on a thumbnail to see a larger version.

Decorative dividers

Long, thin pictures, known as bars, can be used to divide up different sections of information on a Web page.

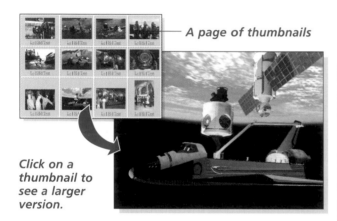

A bar has the same function as a rule but looks more interesting.

Backgrounds

You can use computer graphics to create attractive backgrounds. A background is usually made from a small graphic, called a tile, that a browser displays over and over again.

Patterns that don't distract your visitor's attention from the text, and that fit in well with the theme of the page, look best.

This page has a background that looks like water.

This tile is repeated to create the background.

Indicate links

A picture can be a hyperlink to another·Web page. For example, a picture of a house, such as the ones shown here, is often used as a hyperlink to a site's home page. A small picture that represents the page to which it connects is known as an icon.

A selection of home page icons

Obtaining pictures

There are many pictures on the Web that you can copy and include on your site. You can find collections of backgrounds, bars, buttons and icons. To do this, use a search engine to carry out a key word search (see page 7).

Alternatively, you can visit one of the sites listed on page 41. You will find instructions for copying pictures off the Web onto your computer on page 40.

You will find these icons at http://aplusart.simplenet.com/aplusart/index.html

Copyright

Not all of the pictures on the Web are free for you to use. Much of the information on the Web is "copyrighted". This means a particular person or organization controls the ways in which copies of the information are used.

If you want to put copyrighted information on your Web site, you must first contact the organization that owns the copyright and obtain their permission. If you don't do this, you may be breaking the law.

This sign usually appears on a Web site when the information is copyrighted.

Free information

Some information, known as public domain information, is not copyrighted.

The pictures in the collections listed on page 41 are in the public domain. If you find any other picture collections, make sure the pictures are available for public use before including any of them in your site.

A selection of copyright free images from http://www.nasa.gov/

Digital pictures

You may want to include your own drawings or photographs on your site. Before you do this, you have to record them in digital code. This is a number code that computers can understand. You can only put pictures that are recorded digitally on a Web site.

Pictures can be converted into digital code by a machine called a scanner. This process is called scanning in.

A scanner

You can find out more about it on page 20.

Scanners are quite expensive, but you don't have to buy one. You can have your pictures scanned at most photocopying shops or photograph processing bureaux. Alternatively, you can hire a scanner from a computer hardware shop and scan in your pictures yourself. There is some information about the cost of scanning on page 42.

Preparing pictures

When you scan in a picture, you create an image file that you can insert into a Web page. This section explains how to create image files and adapt them for use on the Web.

How does a scanner work?

A scanner is attached to a computer. Software on the computer tells the scanner how to collect and save information about a picture. This software is known as image-editing or imaging software.

The scanner divides a picture into tiny dots known as picture elements or pixels. It gathers information about the colour and position of each one. It then records this information in digital code so that the computer can reproduce the picture. You use imaging software to tell a scanner how many pixels to divide a picture into. The number of pixels in an image is known as its resolution. It is usually measured in dots per inch (dpi).

Pixels

When you look at a digital image close up, the pixels are clearly visible.

Imaging software also lets you alter or "edit" digital images, and create images from scratch. You can find out how to obtain an image-editing program on pages 40 to 41.

File size

When creating picture files for use on the Web, it is important to make them as small as possible so that they download quickly. The size of a file is measured in bytes.

Resolution

You can control the size of an image file by changing its resolution. A "high" resolution image contains a lot of pixels so it produces a large file. A "low" resolution image contains fewer pixels so it is contained in a smaller file.

You can see the difference between a high resolution and low resolution image when you print them out.

Compare the quality of a high resolution picture to the quality of a low resolution picture.

This is a high resolution image. It was scanned in at 350 dpi.

This is a low resolution image. It was scanned in at 72 dpi.

High resolution and low resolution images look very similar on a computer monitor. When you prepare a picture for use on the Web, scan it in at 72 or 75 dpi. Low resolution images are good enough for use on the Web.

Saving pictures

Imaging software can save pictures in many different ways. The most popular types of picture files used on the Web are Graphical Interchange Format (GIF) and Joint Photographic Experts Group (JPEG) format.

GIF

GIF files are usually used for pictures that have large proportions of one colour, or that are irregularly shaped. For example, most icons, buttons and bars are GIF files.

These icons from the Chicago Museum of Science and Industry's site are GIF files.

GIF files contain a maximum of 256 colours. This helps to make the files small. If a picture contains more than 256 colours, an imaging program reduces the number of colours to save it as a GIF. When you save a picture as a GIF, add the extension **.gif** to the file name.

JPEG format

JPEG files are ideal for pictures that contain many different colours, such as photographs. They record the information in a way that takes up less space. This is called compression.

JPEG files can be compressed by different amounts. The greater the amount of compression, the smaller the size of the file. However, the amount of compression also affects how good a picture looks. The smaller the amount of compression, the better the quality of the picture.

This picture of the Chicago Museum of Science and Industry (http://www.msichicago.org/) is a JPEG file.

Try compressing a file by different amounts until you find the smallest file that still looks good. To do this, first save a few different versions of an image by altering the amount of compression each time. When you save a JPEG file, add the extension **.jpg** to the file name.

A dialog box from an imaging program called Adobe® Photoshop®

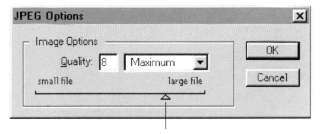

Move this slider to the left to compress the file.

Next, open up all the versions at the same time in your imaging program so that you can compare what they look like. Try to keep all your picture files under 30 kilobytes (KB).

Measurements

When you have inserted a picture into a Web page (see page 22), look at it through your browser. You should be able to see all of it without using the scroll bars.

If necessary, use your imaging program to make a picture smaller. The size of a digital image is measured in pixels. For example, a 40 x 42 icon is 40 pixels across and 42 pixels high. When you resize a picture, make sure you change its height and width in proportion or it will become distorted.

Adding an object, such as a picture or a sound, to a Web page is known as embedding. This section tells you how to embed pictures.

Embedding a picture

Imagine, for example, you want to embed a picture called "martin.jpg" in a Web page. First place the picture file in the same directory as the page's source document on your computer's hard disk. Open up the source document and type <IMG SRC="martin.jpg"> where you want the picture to appear.

You can insert this embedding tag anywhere on a Web page, as long as it is between the two parts of the <BODY> tag.

A Web page containing a picture and its source

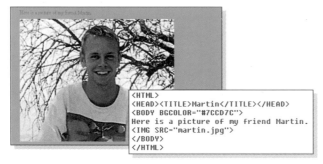

```
<HTML>
<HEAD><TITLE>Martin</TITLE></HEAD>
<BODY BGCOLOR="#7CCD7C">
Here is a picture of my friend Martin.
<IMG SRC="martin.jpg">
</BODY>
</HTML>
```

No pictures

Some people surf the Web with browsers that can't display images. Others instruct their browsers not to display images so they can download pages more quickly.

It is polite to let these people know what the pictures they can't see are like. To do this, you can instruct a browser to display words, known as alternative text, instead of a picture.

Part of Yahoo!'s home page viewed without images

This is alternative text.

Alternative text

To provide alternative text for a picture, add ALT="alternative text" to its embedding tag. For example, the embedding tag for a picture of an oak tree might look like this <IMG SRC="oak.gif" ALT="oak tree">.

Downloading pictures

When you download a page from the Web, the words on the page usually appear on your screen before the pictures. This is because pictures take longer to travel across the Net.

If a browser knows how wide and how high a picture is going to be, it can leave the right amount of space as it displays the text. Otherwise, it may have to rearrange the text on the page when the picture arrives. You can warn a browser how big a picture is by adding extra information to the embedding tag.

This picture is still being downloaded.

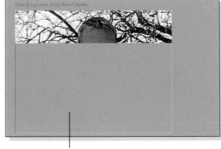

The browser has drawn a box in which the rest of the picture will appear.

To do this, first use your image-editing program to find out the picture's dimensions in pixels. Then you can add this information to the picture's embedding tag.

Imagine, for example, you are using a picture which is 180 pixels across and 140 pixels high. Insert WIDTH=180 HEIGHT=140 into the embedding tag. The embedding tag should now look something like this: <IMG WIDTH=180 HEIGHT=140 SRC="martin.jpg">.

Arranging pictures

To instruct a browser to align a picture left or right, add ALIGN="LEFT" or ALIGN="RIGHT" to the embedding tag. For example, if you wanted to align a picture right, the tag would be similar to this: <IMG WIDTH=180 HEIGHT =180 SRC="bridge.jpg" ALIGN="RIGHT">.

The picture on this page is aligned.

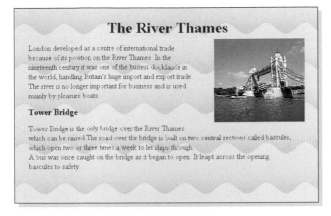

Notice how the picture pushes the text to the left.

You can use the <CENTER> tag (see page 13) to instruct a browser to place a picture in the middle of a page. To do this, place the two parts of the tag around the embedding tag. For example, <CENTER><IMG WIDTH=180 HEIGHT=180 SRC="bridge.jpg"></CENTER>.

When a picture appears in the middle of a Web page, it pushes the text downwards.

Reusing pictures

It is a good idea to reuse pictures wherever possible. This brightens up a site without increasing the time it takes to download.

When a browser downloads a Web page, it copies each piece of information onto your computer. So, when a picture appears for a second time, the browser displays the copy that is stored on your computer. It doesn't have to fetch the information from the Web again.

Several of the pictures on this site are repeated.

Background

To add a patterned background to a page, you need to add some code to the <BODY> tag.

Imagine you want to use a tile called "tile.gif" to form a background for your page. Insert BACKGROUND="tile.gif" in the <BODY> tag, like this: <BODY BGCOLOR ="#FFF8E0" BACKGROUND="tile.gif">.

When you use a patterned background you should also specify a background colour for the page. People whose browsers don't show pictures will see this colour instead.

Linking Web pages

Once you have created a few Web pages, you can join them together with hyperlinks. You can also link your pages to other people's sites.

You can make words or pictures into hyperlinks. For example, you could make a hyperlink to the White House Web site from the sentence "Last year, my family and I visited the White House" or from a photograph of the White House.

Links within a site

Links within a Web site are called local links. They help visitors to find their way around the pages on the site. Each of your pages should contain a link to your home page as well as a selection of links to other pages on your site.

Links to other sites

Links to other sites are known as remote links. You can use remote links to connect your page to other pages on the same subject or to direct your visitors to sites you have enjoyed.

Linking tag

You can turn any word, phrase or picture into a hyperlink by using an "anchor tag".

An anchor tag

`<A HREF="http:www.usborne.co.uk">`

`</A>` —Closing part   Opening part

An anchor tag's opening part tells a browser to download another page and specifies the location of that page. The tag shown above contains a URL. This is because the page to which the link connects belongs to another site.

When you create a local link, the opening part of an anchor tag contains different information. If a page is stored in the same directory, you need only insert its name. For example, <A HREF="music.htm">. If a page is stored in a subdirectory, include the filename and its location. For example, <A HREF="hobbies/music.htm">.

This picture shows how you can use hyperlinks to jump from one Web site to another.

These links are part of the text.

A list of interesting and useful sites is called an index.

Picture links

To create a picture link, place the two parts of the anchor tag around the tag used to embed the picture (see page 22).

Imagine, for example, you want to transform a picture called "balloon.gif" into a link to this page: **http://www.ballooning.co.uk/**. You would type:

<A HREF="http://www.ballooning.co.uk/"> <IMG SRC="balloon.gif"></A>.

Your browser will display the picture with a border. This indicates that it is a link. Remember that some people's browsers are not set up to show pictures (see page 22). Whenever you use a picture as a hyperlink, always provide a text link as well.

Click on the balloon to see a page about ballooning.

Border

Remove a border

If you don't like the border that surrounds a picture link, you can instruct a browser not to display it. To do this, add BORDER=0 to the embedding tag. For example, <IMG BORDER=0 SRC="balloon.gif">.

Visitors to your site will still be able to tell that a picture without a border is a

hyperlink. When they pass their mouse over it, the pointer will change to a hand symbol, like the one shown here.

Text links

To create a text link, place the two parts of the anchor tag around the word or phrase that you want to act as a link. For example, to turn the words "White House" into a link to the White House site at **http://www.whitehouse.gov/**, you would type:<A HREF="http://www.white house.gov/">White House</A>.

Your browser will underline the words White House and display them in a different colour. This makes it clear they form a hyperlink.

Click on the underlined text to go to the White House home page.

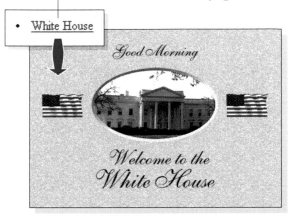

On the Web

The addresses of Web pages can change, and some pages are removed from the Web altogether. As a result, hyperlinks can become out-of-date or "invalid".

When you click on an invalid hyperlink, an error message will appear on your screen to explain that your browser can't find a page at the address indicated in the anchor tag.

Once your site is on the Web, you should regularly check your links to other people's pages. Be sure to update or remove any invalid hyperlinks so that visitors to your site aren't disappointed or frustrated by them.

Including sounds

You can record sounds onto your computer and add them to your Web site. To do this, you may need some extra hardware and software.

Sound hardware

A computer uses a device called a sound card to capture sounds in digital format and play them back. All Macs and multimedia PCs contain sound cards. If you have another kind of computer, you may need to add one. You'll also need headphones or speakers to hear sounds coming from your computer.

Sound card

Speakers

Microphone

To record your own sounds, such as your voice, you will need a microphone that can be plugged into your computer. If you want to record something from a cassette or a CD, you will need a cable to connect your stereo set to your computer.

Ready-made sounds

You may prefer to use ready-made sound clips on your site. You can find collections of sound clips on CD-ROM and on the Web.

Before you add a sound clip to your Web site, make sure it is copyright-free (see page 19), or that you have permission from the person who created the sound.

Sound software

To create your own sound clips, you need a program that allows you to record and edit sound. You may already have such a program on your computer. The example shown below is Sound Recorder, a sound editing program that comes with Windows® 95. If you don't already have a suitable program, or you want a more advanced one, you can download one from the Net (see pages 40-41).

The Sound Recorder window

Click here to start recording a sound.

Click here to stop recording.

Sound file formats

There are several different types of sound files. The ones that are usually used on the Web are: AU, MIDI, WAV and AIFF.

 AU files work on all types of computers, but they sometimes sound a bit crackly.

 MIDI files work on all types of computers and sound better than AU files.

 WAV is the Microsoft® Windows® audio format. Most browsers can handle these files.

 AIFF is the Macintosh audio file format. Most browsers can play these files.

Create a sound clip

Use your sound editing program to record and save a sound in a suitable format. Your program may allow you to choose a recording quality. The higher the quality of the recording, the bigger the sound file will be.

Some sound programs enable you to add special effects or mix sounds together. For example, with Sound Recorder, you can add echoes to your sound or reverse it so that you hear everything backwards.

A dialog box from Sound Recorder

Choose between CD, Radio or Telephone Quality.

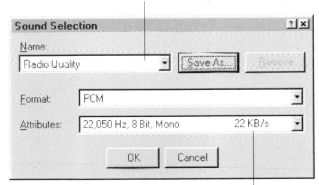

This tells you how many kilobytes (KB) of disk space one second of the selected sound quality requires.

Sound clips on the Web

 Sound files are usually very big files. A few seconds of speech can take up over 100 KB of disk space, even when it is recorded at low quality.

Not all Web users want to spend time downloading sound clips, so it is better to create a hyperlink to a sound file rather than embed it directly in a Web page. Near the hyperlink, you should indicate how big the sound file is, how long it will play for, and what information it contains. This enables visitors to your site to decide whether or not they want to hear the sound clip. If they do, they can click on the hyperlink to download it.

Link to a sound file

You use an anchor tag to link to a sound file. For example, to turn "Listen to me play the drums (150 KB)" into a link to "drum.wav", you would type: <A HREF="drum.wav"> Listen to me play the drums (150 KB)</A>.

When you follow a link to a sound file, a window containing a device called an audio player appears on screen. This plays sound files. Some audio players start automatically. With others, you have to click on a play button.

An audio player

The slider bar moves across as the sound plays.

Embed a sound file

The tag used to insert a sound file into a Web page is: <EMBED SRC="?">. Imagine, for example, you want to embed a sound file called "welcome.wav". To do this you would type: <EMBED SRC="welcome.wav">.

Some browsers will display an audio player in response to this tag. Others will display an icon that you can click on to hear the sound.

Netscape Navigator displays an icon.

The icon

Double-click on the icon to hear the sound.

Moving images

You can make your Web site more eye-catching by adding moving pictures, such as animations.

Animation

An animation is a moving image made from a sequence of pictures, known as frames. Each frame is slightly different from the previous one. When they are displayed in quick succession, the objects in the pictures appear to move.

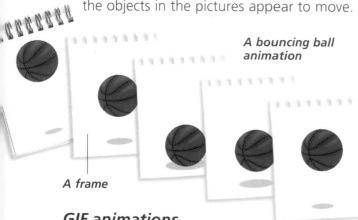

A bouncing ball animation

A frame

GIF animations

A GIF animation is produced from a series of GIF files. GIF animations are very popular on the Web. They are easy to create and any browser that can show GIF files can play GIF animations.

Obtaining GIF animations

On the Web, there are collections of GIF animations that you can use on your Web site for free. To find a GIF animation, perform a search for **animated GIF** or **GIF animation**.

You download and embed GIF animations in the same way as you download and embed ordinary pictures (see pages 22 and 40).

This animation was saved from http://www.webpromotion.com/.

Create your own GIF animations

To create your own GIF animations, you need an imaging program (see page 20) and a "GIF animation editor". This is a program that allows you to build up a sequence of GIF files. (Find out where to obtain one on page 41.)

First plan out your animation on paper. Try to use as few frames as possible to form your animation in order to keep the file size down. It is best not to use more than 12 frames.

Next, create the frames using your imaging program. Save each picture separately in GIF format. When saving animation frames, give each file a name that indicates where it comes in the sequence. This will be helpful when you build up your animation.

If these frames are shown in this order, the clock's hand goes round clockwise.

clock1.gif   clock2.gif   clock3.gif   clock4.gif

If they are shown in reverse order, the clock's hand goes round anti-clockwise.

Build up a GIF animation

Once you have created all the frames for your animation, use your GIF animation editor to bring them together into a single file.

Animation editors let you control the order in which the frames appear, and how many times over the animation will play. Some programs let you specify other information, such as for how long each frame should appear.

Java™ applets

Another way to add animation and sound to a Web page is by embedding a Java™ applet. This is a tiny program written in a computer programming language called Java.

Java applets can contain animation, sound and interactive features. This means you can change things on a Web page by clicking with your mouse. On page 41 there is a list of Web sites where you can find ready-made applets to add to your site.

In this Java applet, the moons whizz around the planet.

Including Java

Web sites that offer free Java applets usually include instructions for embedding them in a Web page.

To see a Java applet in operation, it is best to use Netscape Navigator® 4.03, Microsoft® Internet Explorer 4, or a later version of either of these browsers.

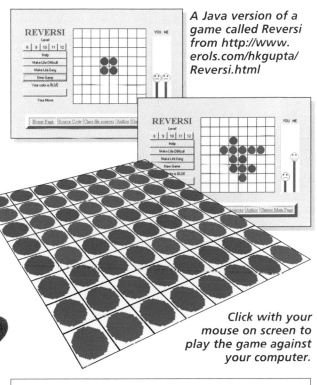

A Java version of a game called Reversi from http://www.erols.com/hkgupta/Reversi.html

Click with your mouse on screen to play the game against your computer.

Video

You can embed a video clip into a Web page in the same way as you add a sound clip. However, video clips are more complicated to create and they produce huge files that you or visitors to your site may have trouble downloading.

As home, school and office computers become more and more powerful, video clips will become more popular with Web site builders and users alike.

Once your site is on the Web, there are ways of finding out how many people visit it and what they think of it.

Keeping count

To find out how popular your site is, you can include a "counter". This is a small program that keeps a running total of the number of times a Web site is visited. In Web jargon, this number is known as a hit count.

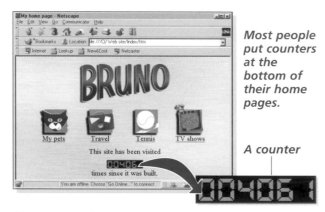

Most people put counters at the bottom of their home pages.

A counter

Free counters

Some Web advertising companies will provide you with a counter for free (see page 41). They keep the counter on their computer and allow you to link your Web site to it.

To obtain a free counter, you have to go to the company's Web site and complete a form similar to the one below.

Part of the form from http://www.pagecount.com/

Counter forms

The form usually asks for information about you and your site. There may also be a section that allows you to select a counter style.

These are some of the counter styles you can choose from at http://www.pagecount.com/.

When you have completed a form, use the *Send* button to return it to the computer it came from. You will then be told exactly what code you need to use to create a link from your home page to your counter.

Some companies send this information straight away on a Web page. Others send an e-mail message (see page 31).

A guest book

A guest book is a device that allows visitors to your site to leave comments about the Web site, and to read the comments left by previous visitors.

On page 41, there is a list of companies that allow you to link to a guest book for free.

⚠ Feedback problems

Free counters and guestbooks are great for personal Web sites. But they aren't totally reliable. They will only function if the computer on which they are stored is working. From time to time, there may be a problem with this computer. Anyone who visits your site at these times will not be counted. They will also not be able to leave a message in your guestbook.

Electronic mail

Electronic mail, or e-mail, is the process of sending messages from one computer to another across a network. Visitors to your site can use e-mail to send you messages. To do this, they will need to know your e-mail address.

The organization that provides you with access to the Net will provide you with an e-mail address. An e-mail address has two main sections: the username and the domain name. These two sections are divided up by an @ symbol. Here is an imaginary e-mail address:

username   at   domain name

To prepare an e-mail, you type your message into a window similar to the one shown in the picture below.

Link to e-mail

Many Net users have separate programs for browsing the Web and sending e-mail. You can make it easy for them to send you messages by including a "mailto" link on your site. This is a link that instructs the browser to start the e-mail program, and open a window containing your e-mail address.

Imagine, for example, that your e-mail address is Webmaster@usborne.co.uk and you want to turn the words "Contact our Webmaster" into a mailto link. You would insert the following code into a source document, <A HREF="mailto:Webmaster@ usborne.co.uk">Contact our Webmaster</A>.

Some Web users' equipment can't handle a mailto link. In order to send a message to you, they will have to copy down your address and type it into their e-mail program. If you want everybody to be able to send you e-mail, make sure you put your e-mail address on your site.

Netscape Messenger's Composition window

The e-mail address of the recipient goes here.

The subject of the message goes here.

The message goes in the body section.

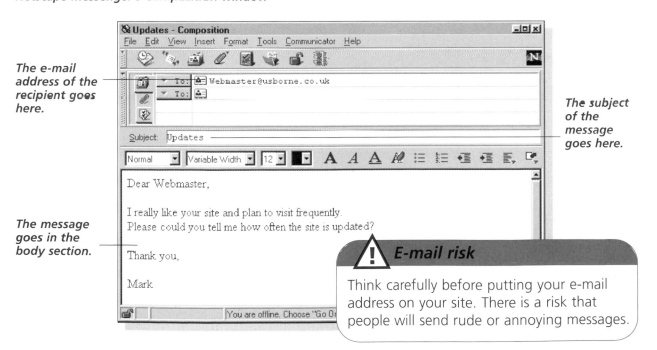

⚠ E-mail risk

Think carefully before putting your e-mail address on your site. There is a risk that people will send rude or annoying messages.

Describing your pages

Most people use programs called search engines to find information on the Web. A search engine looks for pages containing specific words and displays a list of the pages it finds. You can add tags to your page that tell a search engine what information your page contains. These tags are known as meta tags.

Meta tags

The most commonly used meta tags are description meta tags and key words meta tags. A description tag summarizes a page's contents, and a key words tag contains a selection of words that are essential to the content of the page.

Meta tags should be placed between the two parts of the <HEAD> tag at the beginning of a source document. The information inside meta tags will not appear on a Web page.

Description tag

A description tag for a page about dinosaurs might look like this:

```
< META NAME="description" CONTENT="This site contains information for children about dinosaurs, natural history museums with dinosaur exhibits, dinosaur societies, fossils and palaeontology." >
```

To adapt this tag for your own Web pages, change the words between the second pair of quotation marks. Try to think up a short, clear description that is no more than 20 words long.

A Web site about dinosaurs at http://www.dinosauria.com/

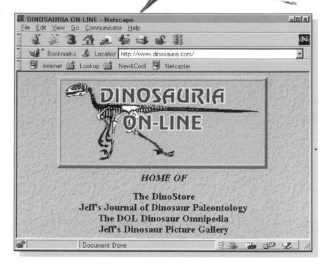

Some of the key words for this site are "dinosaur", "DinoStore" and "Battatt Museum of Science".

Key words tag

Here is a key words tag for an imaginary page about dinosaurs:

```
<META NAME="keywords" CONTENT="dinosaurs, dinosaur, palaeontology, jurassic, natural history" >
```

You can adapt this tag for your own Web pages by replacing the words between the second pair of quotation marks.

How does a search engine work?

When a search engine collects information about a new Web page, it looks for meta tags. If it doesn't find any, it will use its own methods to decide what the page is about. For example, it might display the first few words on a Web page as a description of the page's contents.

Ready for the Web?

Here are some of the things you should do before you put your site on the Web.

Accuracy and efficiency

You should check your site by carefully rereading each page through your browser.

Ensure that all the information on your site is correct and that there are enough local links to enable visitors to find their way around easily (see page 24).

It isn't easy for you to see your site from a visitor's point of view. Things that appear obvious to you, such as where to find a particular piece of information, may not be obvious to others. If possible, ask a friend to explore your site for you. They may be able to suggest some improvements.

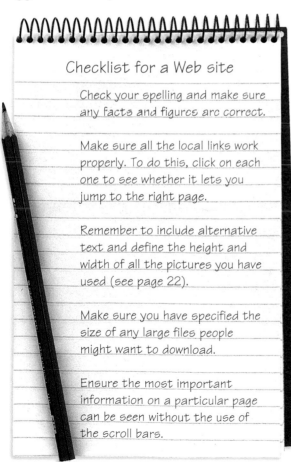

Checklist for a Web site

Check your spelling and make sure any facts and figures are correct.

Make sure all the local links work properly. To do this, click on each one to see whether it lets you jump to the right page.

Remember to include alternative text and define the height and width of all the pictures you have used (see page 22).

Make sure you have specified the size of any large files people might want to download.

Ensure the most important information on a particular page can be seen without the use of the scroll bars.

Filing system

You should store all the files for your Web site in one directory on your computer's hard disk.

If there are a lot of files, you may want to create some subdirectories within your site's main directory. For instance, you could create a subdirectory to hold all the picture files. If you move a file, remember to update the relevant links on your Web pages so that browsers can still locate it. If a browser can't locate a picture file, it displays an icon instead.

This picture shows the icon Netscape Navigator displays when it can't find a picture file.

Use different equipment

A Web page may appear slightly different when it is looked at using a different computer, browser, operating system or type of Net connection. If possible, try out your Web site on a variety of different machines to check that it looks acceptable on all of them.

Finishing touches

It is important to include the date you finished your site so that visitors know how up-to-date the information it contains is.

Finally, make extra copies of all the files and store them in a safe place. That way, if anything happens to the computer to which you transfer your site, you won't have lost all your hard work.

Providing Web space

Web sites are stored on powerful computers called servers or hosts. Before people can visit your site, you will have to transfer it to a Web server. Unless you have your own server, you will need to rent space on someone else's.

A server

A company that rents out space on Web servers is known as a hosting company. There are two main types of hosting companies: Internet access providers and Web presence providers.

Internet access providers

Internet access providers (IAPs) are companies that provide access to the Net, such as Internet service providers (ISPs) and on-line services. An ISP only provides access to the Net, whereas an on-line service also provides access to a private network of information.

Most IAPs provide customers with between 1 and 5 megabytes (MB) of space on a Web server. 1MB is just over a million bytes and is enough to store a small personal Web site.

Web presence providers

Web presence providers are companies that specialize in storing or "hosting" Web sites. They usually offer large amounts of space and extra services such as the ones discussed on pages 38 and 39. Because of this, many of their customers are businesses and big organizations.

These Web presence providers host business Web sites.

Making choices

You can find the addresses of Internet access providers and Web presence providers in Internet magazines or on the Web (see page 42). Each company offers a slightly different service and charges different fees.

Here are some questions that you might like to ask before you choose a company to host your Web site:

How fast will my site download?

Find out how powerful the servers are, and how they are linked to the Net. The more powerful the server, and the greater the bandwidth of the link (see right), the quicker your pages will download.

It's a good idea to visit a hosting company's Web site to see how quickly their own pages download. If they can't deliver their own pages quickly, they are unlikely to be able to offer you a better service.

What extra services do you offer?

Depending on the content of your Web site, you may require some extra services (see pages 38 and 39). For example, if you intend to use your site to sell things, you will need a hosting company that can make it safe for you to use your site to collect private information such as credit card details and telephone numbers.

You may expect a lot of the people that will use your site to access the Net through a type of digital telephone line known as an Integrated Services Digital Network (ISDN) line. If so, you should choose a company that has an ISDN connection to the Internet.

Make sure a hosting company can provide all the extra services you may require.

What costs can I expect?

Make sure you understand exactly how much a company will charge to host your site. Most companies charge a monthly fee and some charge an initial set up fee too.

Hosting companies often offer a variety of deals, each with a different monthly fee. The price you pay will depend on the size of your site, the type of cables the hosting company uses, and any extra services you require.

Are there any extra costs?

Sometimes a monthly fee doesn't include all the services you might require. For instance, a company may charge you extra each time you update your site. Try to find one that will let you change your site as often as you like for no extra cost.

Each time someone visits your site, a certain amount of computer data is copied from the server where your site is stored to their computer. Most of the prices quoted by hosting companies cover a limited amount of data transfer. If a lot of people visit your site or if it contains a lot of very large files, you may exceed this amount. Hosting companies usually record how much data is copied from your site each month and may charge you extra for going over the limit.

Do you provide technical support?

You may need advice on how to transfer your site to the Web and how to maintain it. Find out if a company provides support for its clients and whether this is done by telephone or by e-mail. Make sure support will be available at the times when you are most likely to need it.

Bandwidth

When two or more computers are connected, a channel for exchanging information is formed. The computers on the Net are connected by telephone networks, by fibre optic cables and by satellite. Different types of channel can transfer different amounts of data per second. The maximum amount of data a channel can transfer is known as its bandwidth capability.

Communications satellite

Hosting companies connect their servers to the Net in different ways. In general, hosting companies that use faster channels are more expensive.

Fibre optic cables

Most hosting companies use fibre optic cables to connect their servers to the Internet. These cables contain thin glass strands called optical fibres that carry data. There are four types of fibre optic cables and each type has a different bandwidth. I1 cables can transfer up to 1.5 megabytes of data per second (mbps), T2 can transfer up to 10 mbps, T3 can transfer up to 30 mbps and ATM can transfer up to 100 mbps.

Some hosting companies connect their servers to the Internet by ISDN. ISDN lines have a bandwidth of 128 kilobytes per second (kbps). Web users can only benefit from the speed of ISDN transfer if they use an ISDN line to connect to the Net and a computer with ISDN hardware and software.

This is an ISDN terminal adaptor. It is a device that allows a computer to send and receive data across ISDN lines.

Uploading your site

This section shows you how to transfer your Web site files onto your hosting company's server. Copying files from your computer onto another computer on the Internet is called uploading. Files are usually uploaded using a method called File Transfer Protocol (FTP).

FTP clients

To transfer files by FTP, you need a program called an FTP client. On page 41, there is a list of FTP clients that are available on the Internet.

When you open an FTP client, you will see a window divided into two parts, similar to the one shown below. The left part displays a list of the files that are stored on your computer, called the local computer. The right part is used to display the files that are stored on other computers, known as remote computers.

The first time you open your FTP client the right part of the window will be blank. This is because your computer is not yet connected to a remote computer.

Preparations

In order to upload your site, you have to connect your computer to your hosting company's computer. To instruct your FTP client to do this, you need to enter some information, such as the computer's address, into a dialog box. With WS_FTP, this dialog box appears each time you start the program. Your hosting company will tell you exactly what information you need to enter in order to connect to their computer.

Connecting

Once you have given your FTP client this information, you are ready to connect your computer to the hosting company's server. Connect to the Internet in the usual way. Then click on the *Connect* button in your FTP client. When your FTP client has connected to the server, the files that are stored on the server will appear on the right side of the window.

A window from an FTP client called WS_FTP

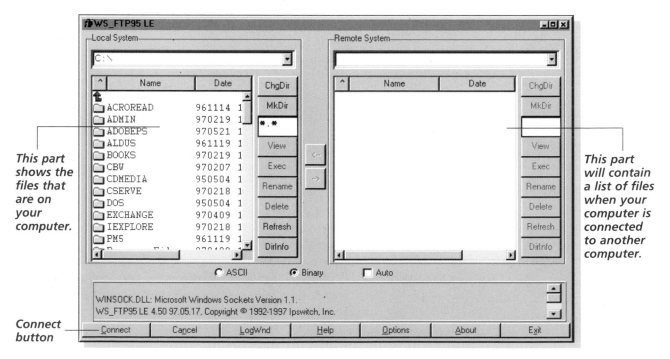

This part shows the files that are on your computer.

This part will contain a list of files when your computer is connected to another computer.

Connect button

Transferring files

First use the left part of your FTP client's window to locate your Web site files on your computer's hard disk. You can open a directory or folder by double-clicking on its icon. Next use the right part of the window to open the directory on the server where you are going to store your Web site. Your hosting company will tell you which directory you should use.

Transferring files with WS_FTP

Use this button to upload files.

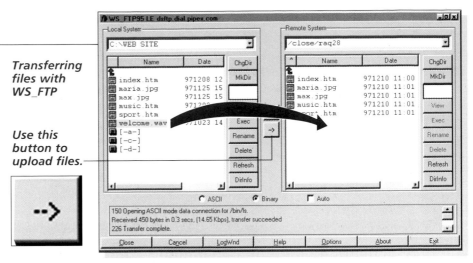

To transfer a file, select its filename with your mouse and click on the button which points to the right. You can select several files at once, but is is safest to transfer files one by one.

When a file has been successfully transferred to the server, its filename will appear in the right part of the window.

As soon as you have finished transferring a file, anyone with access to the Web can look at it as a Web page.

After uploading

Checking hyperlinks
Make sure that all the hyperlinks on your site work properly. To do this, connect to the Internet and download your home page by typing its URL into your browser's *Address* or *Location* box. Your hosting company will tell you what your home page's URL is. Once you have called up your home page, click on each of the links on your site to check it leads to the right page.

Updating your site
To update your Web site, you have to change the source documents that are stored on your computer. When you are happy with the changes, transfer the new version of the files to the server. Your FTP client will automatically use these to replace the old versions.

Publicizing your site
To enable other Web users to find your site, you should tell a selection of search engines about it (see page 43).

To do this, go to a search engine's home page and look for a hyperlink called Add URL or something similar. Click on this link to download a registration form. A search engine will use the information you enter onto its form to find and classify your site.

To avoid repeating this process many times, you can use a service that automatically submits the details of your site to several search services (see page 43).

Hundreds of sites are added to the Web every day. A search engine won't be able to visit your site immediately. You may have to wait several weeks after registration for your site to appear in a search engine's index.

If you are building a Web site to promote the organization you are involved in or to make money, you might like to consider some of the following options.

Advertising

You can make sure people know about your site by advertising it on other Web sites.

Most advertisements on the Web take the form of banners such as the ones shown below. A banner appears at the top of a Web page and is a hyperlink to the advertised site.

A selection of banners

Advertising costs

You can advertise your Web site on other Web sites. There is usually a charge for this. People carry advertisements on their sites so that they can earn money. They can use this money to maintain and improve their sites.

It can be expensive to advertise on very popular sites, such as directories or search engines. Before you pay to advertise on a particular site, ask for information about its visitors. Make sure you choose a site that receives a lot of visits from people who are likely to be interested in your site.

You can advertise for free on some less well-known sites. In return, you have to display advertisements on your site. This is known as a banner exchange.

Forms

Many companies use their Web sites to gather information from visitors. One way to do this is with a form. A form is like a dialog box. It can contain check boxes, lists of options to choose from, and spaces for typing in information.

A form needs a program called a Common Gateway Interface (CGI) script to work. To include a form on your site, you will have to learn how to write CGI scripts or find an expert to help you.

A form from http://www.virginradio.co.uk/

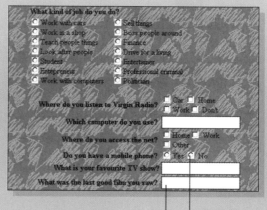

Type in an answer here. ———— A check box

Visitor information

Some hosting companies use software to collect information about the way people explore your site. For example, the software can keep track of how many hits your site receives per hour, which countries the visitors are coming from, and which are the most popular pages on your site.

The information is stored on the Web server in a file known as the statistics log. You can examine your site's statistics log at any time, either by looking at it through your browser or by downloading it via FTP. You may be able to use the information it contains to make your site more efficient.

A search facility

If there are a lot of pages on your Web site, it is a good idea to include a search engine that will search your site for key words.

Search engines are particularly useful on sites that sell things. They enable customers to find what they are looking for quickly and easily. Search engines work using CGI scripts so you may have to find an expert to help you set up a search engine on your Web site.

A search engine from an online bookshop called Amazon at http://www.amazon.com/

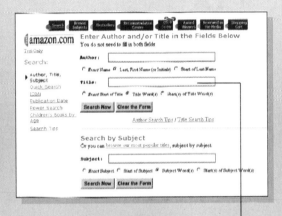

Enter the name of the book you want here.

Security

Many organizations use their Web sites to collect money from customers or donors. The simplest way for Web users to make a payment is by sending their credit card details across the Net. Web users will only do this if there is no risk of anyone else obtaining the information and using it to steal money.

To ensure that it is safe to send private information via e-mail or on a form, the information must be turned into a secret code before it is transferred across the Net. This process is known as encryption. Most hosting companies can arrange for any private information you collect to be encrypted.

Domain names

A Web site's URL always begins with **http://**. This is followed by a section called the domain name.

The URL for the White House Web site

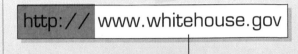

The domain name

Domain names are controlled by organizations called Network Information Centers (NICs). NICs keep a record of all the domain names in use to make sure that a particular name is only used by one organization.

Registering a name

You can personalize the domain name part of your site's URL so that it is easy to remember. You have to pay a NIC for permission to use a particular domain name. This is known as registering. You can find out how much it costs to register a domain name on page 42.

Once you have registered a domain name, you can be sure that it will not be used by any other sites. You can use a registered domain name wherever your site is stored. This means that if you move your site to a different server, it will keep the same URL.

Some hosting companies will register a domain name with an NIC on your behalf. Otherwise, you can contact the NIC for your area directly. You can find the addresses of NIC Web sites on page 43. Many of these sites contain registration forms that you can complete on-line.

These pages tell you where and how to find programs, pictures and other files on the Net, to help you build and maintain your Web site.

Choosing programs

The programs listed on page 41 are grouped according to the functions they perform. There are often several different programs in each category, yet this is just a selection of the programs that are available via the Internet.

Don't be overwhelmed by the choice. There is plenty of information on the Web to help you choose a program. For example, you can read what other people think about a particular program. In the Yahoo! directory, product reviews of software are listed under: **http://www.yahoo.com/Computers_and_ Internet/Software/Reviews/Titles/Internet/**.

Yahoo!'s logo

Alternatively, you can visit the Web sites of on-line computing magazines to find out what experts think (see page 43).

If you're still not sure which program you want, choose one that you can try out free of charge. Once a program's trial period is over, you have to pay for it before you can continue using it.

FTP sites

Software that can be copied off the Internet onto your computer is usually stored on servers known as FTP sites.

You can use your browser to download a program from an FTP site. Many of the Web sites listed here contain a link that allows you to start downloading a particular program. Once you click on a link, you will be guided through the downloading process.

Downloading

In the first stage of the process, you have to provide some information about your computer. You may also be asked to select an FTP site to copy the program from. Choose one in your part of the world so the file downloads as quickly as possible.

Once you have provided all the necessary information, your browser will start downloading the program. After a few seconds, a Save As... dialog box will open. Use this to instruct your browser where to save the program file. While the file is downloading, a File Download window may appear on your screen to keep you informed about the progress of the operation.

File Download window

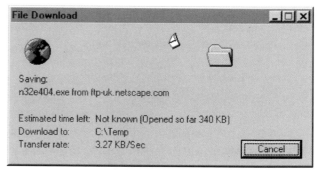

When the program finishes downloading, the window will disappear. Disconnect from the Net before you install the program.

Copying pictures from the Web

To save a picture off the Web, point at it with your mouse and press your mouse button down. If you are using a PC, use the right button. In the menu that appears, select the option called *Save Image As...*, or something similar. A *Save As...* dialog box will appear. Use this to choose a name and location for the picture.

Addresses

Here are the addresses of sites from which you can download software or copy elements, such as pictures and sounds, that you might want to add to your Web pages.

Software

Web editors
Adobe PageMill: **http://www.adobe.com/**
Claris Home Page: **http://www.claris.com/**
DreamWeaver: **http://www.macromedia.com/**

For Windows only:
Hot Dog: **http://www.sausage.com/**
Microsoft® FrontPage®: **http://www.microsoft.com/**

For Macintosh only:
BB Edit: **http://www.barebones.com/**

Image editing software
For Windows only:
L View: **http://www.lview.com/**
JASC's Paintshop Pro: **http://www.jasc.com/**

For Macintosh only:
GraphicConverter: **http://www.goldinc.com/Lemke/**

GIF animation editors
For Windows only:
WebImage **http://www.group42.com/webimage.htm**
Ulead GIF Animator: **http://www.ulead.com/**

For Macintosh only:
GIF Builder: **http://iawww.epfl.ch/Staff/Yves.Piguet/clip2gif-home/GifBuilder.html**

Sound editing programs
CoolEdit: **http://www.syntrillium.com/**
Cubase: **http://www.steinberg.net/**
Mixman Studio: **http://www.mixman.com/**
A site for downloading all kinds of sound software: **http://www.hitsquad.com/**

FTP Clients
For Windows only:
WS_FTP: **http://www.ipswitch.com/**
CuteFTP: **http://www.cuteftp.com/**

For Macintosh only:
Fetch: **http://www.dartmouth.edu/pages/softdev/**

Decompression programs
For Windows only:
PKZip: **http://www.pkware.com/**
Winzip: **http://www.winzip.com/**

For Macintosh only:
StuffIt: **http://www.aladdinsys.com/**

Other
Netscape Navigator®: **http://www.netscape.com/**
Microsoft® Internet Explorer: **http://www.microsoft.com/**

InfoLink, a link checker: **http://www.biggbyte.com/**

Web resources

Pictures and animations:
http://www.w3.org/Icons/
http://www.barrysclipart.com/
http://vr-mall.com/anigifpd/anigifpd.html

Backgrounds:
http://www.netscape.com/assist/net_sites/bg/backgrounds.html
http://www.meat.com/textures/

Java applets
http://javaboutique.internet.com/
http://www.developer.com/directories/pages/dir.java.html

Sounds:
http://www.sounddogs.com/
http://www.microsoft.com/gallery/files/sounds/default.htm

Colour codes:
http://www.imagitek.com/hex
http://www.prgone.com/colors/
http://aloe.com/colors.htm

Counters and guestbooks:
http://www.pagecount.com/
http://www.freecount.com/
http://www.guestworld.com/

Once you have an Internet connection, it is possible to build and maintain a simple Web site at very little extra cost. However, if you choose to add certain features, you will encounter additional costs.

This section provides details about some of the services mentioned in this book. There is also a table showing approximately how much you should expect to pay for these services.

Scanning pictures

The cost of scanning a picture depends on the resolution at which it is scanned. The prices shown in the table are for a low resolution, colour scan of a picture (see page 20). If you have several pictures scanned at once, you may be able to get a discount.

Most places that scan pictures expect you to bring a floppy disk with you. Once they have scanned in your pictures, they will transfer the files onto the disk so you can take them home.

You will usually be asked to leave the pictures and the floppy disk at the bureau and return later to collect your scans. If you have only one picture to scan, you may find that someone is able to do it while you wait.

An Internet connection

Most Internet access providers offer unlimited access to the Internet for a set fee per month. This fee usually includes 1-5 MB of space on a Web server. However, it will not include the cost of any telephone calls that you make when you dial up a connection to their server.

If you already use a company that does not offer free Web space, you may wish to change to one that does. You can find advertisements for access providers in your area in Internet magazines. Alternatively you could visit The Directory for links to the sites of IAPs worldwide. It's at:
http://www.thedirectory.org/

Free Web space

If you use the Internet at school or through a cybercafe, you probably won't have your own account with an Internet access provider. This doesn't prevent you from obtaining free space on a Web server. There are several companies that provide free space for non-commercial Web sites (sites that belong to people who don't wish to make money through the Web). Here is a selection:
http://www.geocities.com/
http://www.fortunecity.com/
http://www.yi.com/

Domain name registration

Different Network Information Centers (see page 37) have different structures of costs for their domain name registration services. In most countries, NICs charge an initial registration fee, as well as an annual renewal fee that ensures that your domain name stays on the register. For example, in the United Kingdom, the initial registration fee is £80. This reserves a domain name for 2 years. After two years, it costs £40 a year to keep the service.

This table shows the approximate cost of the services.

	Unlimited Internet access (per month)	Scanning (per picture)	Domain name registration (per year)
AUS $	50	45	free
CAN $	25	25	free
NZ $	45	5	50
UK £	12	10	40
US $	20	10	50

Useful addresses

Here is a selection of sites that you might find useful as you build your Web site.

Sites for registering a domain name

Australia:
http://www.aunic.net/

Canada:
http://www.cdnnet.ca/

Channel Islands:
http://www.isles.net/

India:
http://ece.iisc.ernet.in/innic/domain.info.html

Ireland:
http://www.ucd.ie/hostmaster/ie-dom.html

Isle of Man:
http://www.nic.im/

Hong Kong:
http://www.apnic.net/

New Zealand:
http://www2.waikato.ac.nz/isocnz/nz-domain/

Malaysia:
http://www.mynic.net/

Singapore:
http://www.nic.net.sg/

South Africa:
http://www.frd.ac.za/uninet/zadomains.html

United Kingdom:
http://www.nic.uk/

USA:
http://www.internic.com/

Non-profit making organizations:
http://rs.internic.net/rs-internic.html

Links to NIC sites for other countries:
http://www.uninett.no/navn/domreg.html

Search services

Altavista:
http://www.altavista.digital.com/

HotBot:
http://www.hotbot.com/

Lycos:
http://www.lycos.com/

OpenText:
http://www.opentext.com/

WebCrawler:
http://www.webcrawler.com/

Yahoo!:
http://www.yahoo.com/

Search engines for software:
http://www.shareware.com/
http://www.download.com/

Site that submit URLs to search services:
http://www.submit-it.com/
http://www.powerpromote.com/

Computing magazines

PC Magazine Online:
http://www.zdnet.com/pcmag/

ZDNet Mac:
http://www.zdnet.com/mac/

C/Net:
http://www.cnet.com/

Web site design tutorials

Beginners:
http://werbach.com/barebones/
http://www.w3.org/MarkUp/
http://www.pageresource.com/

Advanced:
http://www.quadzilla.com/
http://www.webcoder.com/

Glossary

abc Here is a list that explains some of the words you may come across while you are building your Web site. Any word that appears in *italic* type is defined elsewhere in this glossary.

AIFF A sound *file format* developed by a company called Apple Computers.

alternative text Text that a *browser* displays instead of a picture.

anchor tag An *HTML* instruction used to create *hyperlinks*.

animation A moving image made by playing a series of pictures in quick succession.

applet A small program written in *Java*.

AU A sound *file format*.

audio player A program that plays sounds.

backup A copy of a computer program or a computer document.

bandwidth A measurement of the amount of data that can flow through a link between computers. It is usually measured in *bps*.

bar A long, thin picture used to divide up information on a *Web page*.

bit The smallest unit of computer data.

block quote tag An *HTML* instruction used to distinguish quotations from the main text on a *Web page*.

block level element A *tag* that is automatically followed by a paragraph break.

bps (*bits* per second). The unit used to measure how fast data is transferred.

browser A program that enables you to look at documents on the *Web*.

byte A unit of eight *bits*.

case-sensitive A word used to describe a program that is able to distinguish between capital and small letters.

CGI script (Common Gateway Interface script). A type of program that processes information entered into a *form*. It may automatically create *Web pages* in response to this information.

client A program that enables a computer to use the services provided by other computers.

clip art Pictures that are publicly available for illustrating computer documents.

compression Converting a file to a format that minimizes the amount of space it takes up on a disk.

computer graphics Pictures created with a computer.

counter A device that counts how many times a *Web page* is *downloaded* by *Internet* users.

digital A word used to describe information that is recorded as a number code that can be understood and processed by computers. It is also used to describe a device, such as a computer, that can process this number code.

digitize The process of converting information into number code that can be processed by computers.

domain name A name that identifies a particular *Internet* computer.

dots per inch A measure of *resolution*.

download To copy a file from a computer on the *Internet* to your computer.

e-mail (electronic mail). The process of sending a message from one computer to another across a *network*.

embed To place an object such as a picture or sound in a computer document.

encryption The process of converting a message into a code to keep information secret.

expansion card A device, such as a *sound card*, that extends a computer's capabilities by enabling it to perform a particular task.

file format The way a program stores information on a disk.

form A whole or part of a *Web page* that works like a questionnaire. Information can be supplied either by typing it into boxes or by selecting from a number of given choices.

frame One of a series of images that makes up an *animation*.

FTP (File Transfer Protocol). A method used to exchange files via the *Internet*.

FTP client A program that enables you to contact another computer on the *Internet* and exchange files with it.

GIF (Graphical Interchange Format). The most popular picture *file format* used for *computer graphics* on *Web pages*.

guestbook A device that allows visitors to a *Web site* to leave comments.

hardware The equipment that makes up a computer or *network*.

home page Also known as a **welcome page**. A page designed as a point of entry into a *Web site*.

host A computer on a *network* that stores files and makes them available to users.

HTML (HyperText MarkUp Language). The code used to turn an ordinary text document into a document that can be displayed by a *browser*.

hyperlink Also known as an **anchor**. A word, phrase or picture on a *Web page* that, when clicked, instructs a *browser* to display another Web page.

in-line image A picture that appears on a *Web page*.

Internet The worldwide computer *network* that is made up of many smaller networks.

Internet access provider (IAP) A company that sells *Internet* connections.

Internet service provider (ISP) A company that sells *Internet* connections.

invalid A word used to describe an out-of-date *hyperlink* or incorrect *HTML*.

imaging software Software that allows you to create and edit *digital* images.

ISDN (Integrated Services Digital Network). A method of sending computer data across *digital* telephone networks.

JPEG format (Joint Photographics Expert Group). A picture *file format* that is usually used for images with a wide range of colours.

key word A word that is essential to a document's content.

kilobyte Approximately 1,000 *bytes*.

link checker A program that tests *hyperlinks* to find out whether they are still valid.

local system The computer at which a user is working, as opposed to a *remote* system.

log off To disconnect from a *network*.

log on To connect to a *network*.

mbps Megabytes per second.

meta tag A *tag* that helps a *search engine* classify a *Web page*.

microphone A device that converts sound into electrical signals that can be processed by a computer.

MIDI (Musical Instrument Digital Interface). A method for the exchange of information between computers and electronic musical instruments.

modem A device that allows computer data to be sent down a telephone line.

network A number of computers and other devices that are linked together so that they can share information and equipment.

NIC (Network Information Center). An organization that controls *domain names*.

off-line Not connected to the *Internet*.

on-line Connected to the *Internet*.

on-line service A company that provides access to a private *network* of information as well as the *Internet*.

ordered list A numbered list on a *Web page*.

pixel (picture element). A tiny dot that is part of a picture. Everything that appears on a computer screen is made up of pixels.

platform A combination of the type of *hardware* a computer is made from, such as IBM PC compatible or Macintosh, and the type of operating system that controls it, such as Windows or Mac OS.

plug-in A piece of *software* that you can add to a *browser* to enable it to perform extra functions, such as displaying video clips.

public domain information Information that anyone can use because it does not belong to a particular person or organization.

remote system The computer to which a user is connected by a *modem* and a telephone line.

resolution The number of *pixels* that make up a picture on a computer screen.

scanner A device that *digitizes* pictures and stores them as computer files.

search engine A program within a *Web page* that locates Web pages containing particular words or phrases.

security The protection of information so that unauthorized users can't look at it or copy it.

server A computer that carries out tasks for other computers on a *network*. For example, some servers store information that all the computers on the network use.

software Programs that allow computers to carry out certain tasks.

sound card A device that enables a computer to capture sound and play it back.

source The *HTML* code that makes up a particular *Web page*.

stale link A *hyperlink* to a document that has been deleted or moved.

statistics log A record of information about the way a particular *Web site* is used. It is stored on the same computer as the Web site.

tag An *HTML* instruction that tells a *browser* how to display a certain part of a document.

terminal adaptor A device that connects a computer or a fax machine to an *ISDN* system.

text editor A program that can produce text documents.

text level element A *tag* that affects the appearance of a piece of text on a *Web page*.

tiling The repeated use of a small picture to fill a larger space.

title The part of a Web page which appears in the title bar of a browser window.

URL (Uniform Resource Locator). The specific address of a resource on the *Internet*.

unordered list A list on a *Web page* that appears with bullet points.

upload To copy files, via the *Internet*, from your computer to another computer.

validator A program that tests *HTML* to see whether it is correct or not.

video card Also known as a **graphics card**. A device that enables a computer to show text and pictures on its screen.

virus A program that interrupts the normal functioning of computer *software* or *hardware*.

WAV A sound *file format* developed by a company called Microsoft.

Webmaster A person who builds or maintains a *Web site*.

Web editor Also known as an **HTML editor.** A program that helps to create *Web pages*.

Web page A computer document written in *HTML* and linked to other computer documents by *hyperlinks*.

Web site A collection of *Web pages*, set up by an organization or an individual, that are usually stored on the same computer.

word processing program A program that can produce text documents with complex layouts and different styles of letters.

World Wide Web Also known as the **Web** or **WWW**. A huge collection of information available on the *Internet*. The information is divided up into *Web pages* which are joined together by *hyperlinks*.

Index

Acknowledgements

Every effort has been made to trace the copyright holders of the material in this book. If any rights have been omitted, the publishers offer their sincere apologies and will rectify this in any subsequent editions following notification.

Usborne Publishing Ltd. has taken every care to ensure that the instructions contained in this book are accurate and suitable for their intended purpose. However, they are not responsible for the content of, and do not sponsor, any Web site not owned by them, including those listed below, nor are they responsible for any exposure to offensive or inaccurate material which may appear on the Web.

Microsoft, Microsoft Windows, Microsoft Internet Explorer and Microsoft FrontPage Express are registered trademarks of Microsoft Corporation in the United States and other countries. Screen shots and icons reprinted with permission from Microsoft Corporation.

Netscape, Netscape Navigator and the Netscape N logo are registered trademarks of Netscape Communications Corporation in the United States and other countries. Netscape Messenger and Netscape Composer are also trademarks of Netscape Communications Corporation, which may be registered in other countries.

Photographs

Cover (and pp2 and10) Gateway P5-200 Multimedia PC. Photograph reproduced with permission from Gateway 2000.
Bon Jovi. ©London Features International Ltd.
Surfer. ©The Telegraph Colour Library/R. Brown.
p2 Animatronic robotic dinosaur. The Natural History Museum London. **http://www.nhm.ac.uk/**
p3 Globe. ©NOAA/Science Photo Library.
p10 Apple Power Macintosh 4400 used by permission of Apple Computer UK Ltd.
p16 Snowflakes. ©Scott Camazine/Science Photo Library.
p17 Droeshout engraving of Shakespeare. Bodleian Library Arch. Gc.8.
p19 Epson GT-9500 flatbed scanner. Used with permission.
p26 Sound card, speakers and microphone used by permission of Creative Labs. **http://www.soundblaster.com/**
p34 Hewlett-Packard NetServer Storage System/6. Used by permission of Hewlett-Packard.
p35 Satellite. ©Science Photo Library. Cables. ©Phillip Hayson/Science Photo Library. Terminal adaptor. 3 Com Impact IQ II. Used with the permission of 3 Com Corporation.
http://www.3com.com/

Screen shots

Cover James' home page. With thanks to James Blake.
http://www.tiac.net/users/loosey/james.html
Space station. Copyright ©1997 Pixelwings, Wize and Dertshei.
Artemis Interactive. Copyright © Artemis Communications Ltd. 1998. **http://www.artemisia.com/**
Cover (and p24) UnderWater World at Mall of America.
http://www.underwaterworld.com/
Cover (and p25) The White House. **http://www.whitehouse.gov/**
p3 Leo Electron Microscopy. Used with permission.
http://www.leo-em.co.uk/
Cyberkids. Cyberkids graphic reprinted with permission from Mountain Lake Software, Inc. **http://www.cyberkids.com/**
Portuguese Air Force site. Used with permission.
http://www.emfa.pt/
Ballet site. Used with permission. **http://www.ballet.co.uk/**
Dinosauria On-line. Copyright ©1995-1998 Jeff Poling. Illustrations by Joe Tucciarone. **http://www.dinosauria.com/**
Hampton Court Palace. Used with permission.
http://buckinghamgate.com/ (Henry VIII image from **http://www.pdimages.com/**)

p4 The Santilli Family Home Page. Used with permission. The Summer Tree. Used with permission.
http://gulf.uvic.ca/~jgrant/tree.html
Peugeot France. Used with permission. **http://www.peugeot.fr/**
"The Simpsons"™. © Twentieth Century Fox Film Corporation. All Rights Reserved. **http://www.foxworld.com/simpindx.htm**
Homework Help. © Copyright 1997 Star Tribune. All rights reserved. **http://www.startribune.com/homework/**
Unicef. Used with permission. **http://www.unicef.org/**
Swedish Royal Family site. All right reserved by the Royal Court of Sweden. © Telia Internet. **http://www.royalcourt.se/**
p4 (and p38) Virgin Radio form. Copyright © Virgin Radio. Used with permission. **http://virginradio.co.uk/**
p7 Hotdog Express. The Hotdog Web Editor is a registered trademark of Sausage Software. **http://www.sausage.com/**
p10 (and pp22, 38 and 40) Yahoo! Text and artwork copyright © by YAHOO! Inc. All rights reserved. YAHOO! and the YAHOO! logo are trademarks of YAHOO! Inc. **http://www.yahoo.com/**
p18 Thumbnails. With thanks to NASA. **http://www.nasa.gov/**
U.S. Navy. Used with permission. **http://www.navy.com/**
p21 Museum of Science and Industry, Chicago. Copyright Musum of Science and Industry, Chicago, USA.
http://www.msichicago.org/
Adobe Photoshop. Adobe and Photoshop are trademarks of Adobe Systems Incorporated. **http://www.adobe.com/**
p23 Group 42. Used with permission. **http://group42.com/**
p24 Aquarium du Québec. Used with permission.
http://www.aquarium.qc.ca/
Aquarium de San Sebastiàn. Used with permission.
http://www.paisvasco.com/cultura/aquarium/
p25 Aerosaurus and Exeter Balloons. Used with permission.
p28 Hand animation created by Webpromotion.com.
© Webpromotion, Inc.
p29 Java and all Java-based trademarks and logos are trademarks or registered trademarks of Sun Microsystems, Inc. in the United States and other countries.
Java planets. Used with the permission of WebTamers.
http://www.webtamers.com/
Reversi game. Used with the permission of Hridayesh K Gupta.
hkgupta@erols.com
p30 Pagecount. Used with permission.
http://www.pagecount.com/
p32 Dinosauria On-line. Copyright ©1995-1998 Jeff Poling. Illustrations by Joe Tucciarone. **http://www.dinosauria.com/**
p34 IBM Global Network. **http://www.ibm.com/**
UUNET. **http://www.uu.net/**. IneXT. **http://www.inext.fr/**. One-O. **http://www.one-o.com/**
p36-37 WS_FTP Limited Edition ©1991-1998 Ipswitch, Inc.. Used with permission. **http://www.ipswitch.com/**
p38 Banners. Used with permission of RapidSite, Inc.
http://www.rapidsite.net/ and British Airways
http://www.british-airways.com/. British Airways advertisement designed by Agency.com.
p39 Amazon. Used by permission of Amazon.com.

With thanks to Dave Evon, Yves Girardin, Martin Hookham, Takashi Kumon, Bob Lancaster, David G Lindgren and Joe Pedley.

First published in 1998 by Usborne Publishing, Ltd, Usborne House, 83-85 Saffron Hill, London EC1N 8RT, England. Copyright ©1998 Usborne Publishing Ltd. The name Usborne and the device ꝏ are Trade Marks of Usborne Publishing Ltd. *All rights reserved.* No part of this publication may be reproduced, stored in a retrieval system or transmitted in any form or by any means, electronic, mechanical, photocopying, recording or otherwise without the prior permission of the publisher.
First published in 1998.
Printed in Spain.